ADVENTURES

Pirate Jack
and the
Inca Treasure

by Leslie Melville and Fabiano Fiorin

W

FRANKLIN WATTS
LONDON•SYDNEY

This is a story about pirates, but Cocos Island is a real island in the Pacific Ocean, off the coast of Costa Rica. Now, it is a national park, famous for its wildlife. But Cocos Island is also famous for its legends of buried pirate treasure, including treasure from Peru, the home of the Incas.

First published in 2010 by
Franklin Watts
338 Euston Road
London NW1 3BH

Franklin Watts Australia
Level 17/207 Kent Street
Sydney NSW 2000

Text © Leslie Melville 2010
Illustrations © Fabiano Fiorin 2010

The rights of Leslie Melville to be identified as the author
and Fabiano Fiorin as the illustrator of this Work have been asserted
in accordance with the Copyright, Designs and Patents Act, 1988.

A CIP catalogue record for this book is available
from the British Library.

ISBN 978 0 7496 9438 8 (hbk)
ISBN 978 0 7496 9444 9 (pbk)

Series Editor: Jackie Hamley
Series Advisor: Catherine Glavina
Series Designer: Peter Scoulding

Printed in China

Franklin Watts is a division of
Hachette Children's Books,
an Hachette UK company
www.hachette.co.uk

Once upon a time there lived a sly pirate captain called Jack.

He and his crew sailed the seas looking for treasure and ships to steal.

But Captain Jack never wanted to share any treasure with the rest of his pirates.

One day, Jack's ship was sailing near to Cocos Island.

He had a treasure map, and he knew that there was a secret hoard of treasure hidden deep in a cave behind a waterfall.

People had told Jack that in the cave there was gold, silver and a magical sword that used to belong to Pachacuti, a famous Inca warrior king.

Captain Jack thought of a plan
so that he could have the treasure
all to himself.

"We shall stop here, lads!" he yelled
to the rest of the pirates. "We need
some fresh drinking water."

Late that night, when Captain Jack thought everyone was asleep, he lowered a boat and rowed ashore. But he was being watched.

"I'll bet that scurvy dog is up to no good," said one of the pirates. "Let's follow him and find out," said the other.

Captain Jack landed on the island and made his way to the secret treasure cave.

He splashed through the waterfall
and squeezed into the hidden
cave entrance.

Glistening in the moonlight lay
Pachacuti's magical sword and
many other treasures.

Jack put the sword in his belt, clutched some coins close to his chest and made his way out of the cave.

The two pirates who had
followed him were waiting on
the other side of the waterfall.
"Hello, Jack," said one. "We
wondered where you were going."

"Seems as though we have some treasure to share," chuckled the other, "while you walk the plank!"

The pirates uncoiled a length of rope and took the coins from their captain. But they did not see the sword in their captain's belt.

21

Quick as a flash, Captain Jack raised the sword high in the air and cried out, "Pachacuti! Pachacuti! Pachacuti!"

In that moment, the
two pirates dropped
the coins and froze.
Then, before Jack's eyes,
they both turned to stone.

Terrified by what he had seen, Captain Jack picked up the coins and took everything back to the treasure cave. Then he raced back to his ship.

The next morning, Jack sailed away. He left two tall stones, that were once cut-throat pirates, standing on the island – and there they remain to this very day!

Puzzle 1

Put these pictures in the correct order.
Which event do you think is most important?
Now try writing the story in your own words!

Puzzle 2

1. Pachacuti! Pachacuti! Pachacuti!

2. No one will notice I've gone.

3. This magic scares me!

4. Let's follow him and see where he goes.

5. Has he got a treasure map on him?

6. I can have all the treasure for myself!

Choose the correct speech bubbles for the characters above. Can you think of any others? Turn over to find the answers.

Answers

Puzzle 1

The correct order is: 1c, 2f, 3a, 4e, 5b, 6d

Puzzle 2

Captain Jack: 1, 2, 3, 6

Pirate crew: 4, 5

Look out for more Hopscotch Adventures: